FOUR PICTURES BY EMILY CARR

NICOLAS DEBON

To Marie

This book is based on *The Complete Writings of Emily Carr* as well as several books about her life and work, especially *The Life of Emily Carr* by Paula Blanchard, *The Art of Emily Carr* by Doris Shadbolt and *Emily Carr: A Biography* by Maria Tippett. Dialogue and events are mostly based on fact although they have been invented in a few instances.

Groundwood Books / Douglas & McIntyre
720 Bathurst Street, Suite 500, Toronto, Ontario
Distributed in the USA by Publishers Group West
1700 Fourth Street, Berkeley, CA 94710

We acknowledge for their financial support of our publishing program the Canada Council for the Arts, the Government of Canada through the Book Publishing Industry Development Program (BPIDP), the Ontario Arts Council and the Government of Ontario through the Ontario Media Development Corporation's Ontario Book Initiative.

ONTARIO ARTS COUNCIL
CONSEIL DES ARTS DE L'ONTARIO

National Library of Canada Cataloging in Publication
Debon, Nicolas
Four Pictures by Emily Carr / by Nicolas Debon.
ISBN 0-88899-532-6
1. Carr, Emily, 1871-1945–Juvenile literature. 2. Painters–Canada–Biography–Juvenile literature. I. Title.
ND249.C3D42 2003   j759.11   C2003-900369-8

Library of Congress Control Number: 2003100429

Nicolas Debon's illustrations are done in gouache and India ink on Arches cold-pressed watercolor paper.

Printed and bound in China

Page 4: *Emily Carr in her Studio* (c. 1936)
Photo by Harold Mortimer Lamb
British Columbia Archives,
D-06009

Page 5: *Ada and Louisa Outside Cedar Canim's House, Ucluelet* (1898-1899)
Watercolor, 17.9 x 26.5 cm
British Columbia Archives,
PDPO2158

Page 11: *Autumn in France* (1911)
Oil on cardboard, 49 x 65.9 cm
National Gallery of Canada, Ottawa, purchased 1948

Page 17: *Silhouette No. 2* (1930-1931)
Oil on cotton duck, 130.2 x 86.5 cm
Vancouver Art Gallery, Emily Carr Trust, 42.3.7 (Photo: Trevor Mills)

Page 23: *Scorned as Timber, Beloved of the Sky* (1935)
Oil on canvas, 112 x 68.9 cm
Vancouver Art Gallery, Emily Carr Trust, 42.3.15 (Photo: Trevor Mills)

Endpapers: Sketches of Indian Artifacts
Pencil on paper
British Columbia Archives,
PDPO0831

Illustrations were partly inspired by the following paintings:
p. 14: *Bathsheba Bathing*, by Rembrandt Van Rijn [1654], Musée du Louvre, Paris, France; *The Lacemaker*, by Jan Vermeer [c.1664], Musée du Louvre, Paris, France; p. 15: *Three Graces*, by Harry W. Phelan Gibb [c.1909], Lucy Wertheim Bequest Collection, Towner Art Gallery, Eastbourne, England; *Portrait de Madame Matisse à la raie verte*, by Henri Matisse [1905], Statens Museum for Kunst, Copenhaguen, Denmark; *Three Women*, by Pablo Picasso [1908], the Hermitage Museum, St. Petersburg, Russia; pp. 19-20: *War Canoes (Alert Bay)*, by Emily Carr [1912], private collection; *Skidegate*, by Emily Carr [1912], The Vancouver Art Gallery; *Tanoo*, *Queen Charlotte Islands*, by Emily Carr [1913], British Columbia Archives; *Indian House Interior with Totems*, by Emily Carr [c.1912-13], The Vancouver Art Gallery; pp. 21-22: *Pic Island*, by Lawren S. Harris [c.1924], The McMichael Canadian Art Collection, Kleinburg, Ontario; *Northern Autumn*, by Lawren S. Harris [1922], London Regional Art and Historical Museums, London, Ontario; *Mount Temple*, by Lawren S. Harris [c.1925], The Montreal Museum of Fine Arts; *North Shore, Lake Superior*, by Lawren S. Harris [1926], The National Gallery of Canada, Ottawa; *Morning Light, Lake Superior*, by Lawren S. Harris [c.1927], MacDonald Stewart Art Centre, Guelph, Ontario; *Lake Superior Island*, by Lawren S. Harris [c.1923], The McMichael Canadian Art Collection, Kleinburg, Ontario; *Northern Lake*, by Lawren S. Harris [c.1923], The McMichael Canadian Art Collection, Kleinburg, Ontario; *The Ice House*, by Lawren S. Harris [c.1923], The McMichael Canadian Art Collection, Kleinburg, Ontario; *Mount Robson*, by Lawren S. Harris [c.1929], The McMichael Canadian Art Collection, Kleinburg, Ontario; p. 24: *Indian Church*, by Emily Carr [1929], The Art Gallery of Ontario, Toronto; *Indian Hut, Queen Charlotte Islands*, by Emily Carr [c.1930], The National Gallery of Canada, Ottawa.

FOUR PICTURES BY EMILY CARR

NICOLAS DEBON

Douglas & McIntyre   A Groundwood Book   Toronto Vancouver Berkeley

Emily Carr (1871-1945)

The youngest of five sisters, Emily Carr was born in Victoria, British Columbia in 1871. A brother was born several years later. Like many children of their time, Emily and her siblings were raised in a strict, formal home with plenty of religious education and prayer.

As a young child Emily (or "Millie" as she was often called) had a strong independent personality. Surrounded by the rugged beauty of Canada's West Coast, she developed a passion for the wilderness and for animals which was to last all her life. She loved to draw and began to take art lessons when she was eight years old. At nineteen or twenty, she went to study art in San Francisco.

Year after year Emily's paintings became increasingly innovative and daring. Sadly, the more unique her style became, the less understanding she received from her family, friends and the conservative citizens in her hometown of Victoria.

Emily treasured the times she was able to be among the native people of the West Coast. These people and their art seemed to give her insights into the meaning of existence that she had not found in her own society.

In the many pages she wrote toward the end of her life, Emily often refers to a sense of spiritual unity between inanimate things and living beings, between art and nature, between religion and art.

Emily Carr was an extraordinarily gifted artist and she is all the more remarkable for being one of the very few women painters of her time. In the face of many challenges she pursued her own vision, basing her work on her great sense of curiosity and respect for the world surrounding her rather than on what was fashionable among artists of the period.

At the age of twenty-seven Emily made a first
sketching trip to a remote native village on the
coast of Vancouver Island. Although racism and
prejudice toward native people were widespread
at the time, Emily did not share in such views.
On the contrary, she was thrilled to be able to
engage in her life-long fascination with West Coast
aboriginal culture. Expedition after expedition, she
slowly built up an extraordinary collection of paintings depicting the richness of West Coast native
life and art.

CEDAR HOUSE

OFF VANCOUVER ISLAND, BRITISH COLUMBIA, APRIL 1899.

WHAT'S A YOUNG LADY LIKE YOU DOING IN SUCH A FARAWAY PLACE?

MY FRIEND WORKS AT THE CHRISTIAN MISSION IN UCLUELET. I'M GOING TO JOIN HER FOR THE SUMMER...

... I CAN'T WAIT TO PAINT THE INDIAN WAY OF LIFE.

ALL YOU'LL FIND HERE IS A BUNCH OF MISERABLE PEOPLE... TOO MUCH DRINKING, NO WORK AND PLENTY OF SICKNESS...

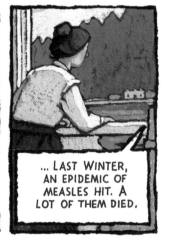

... LAST WINTER, AN EPIDEMIC OF MEASLES HIT. A LOT OF THEM DIED.

WILLAPA

... HERE'S THE EASIEST WAY TO GET TO THE MISSION, MISS.

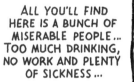

EMILY, HOW GOOD TO SEE YOU!

COME AND HAVE SOMETHING TO EAT.

I HOPE YOU WON'T MIND SITTING ON THIS CRATE... WE ONLY HAVE TWO CHAIRS.

"OUR BLESSED LORD, WE THANK THEE FOR ALL THY MERCIES, FOR THE FOOD..."

"... THAT NOURISHES OUR BODIES..."

THIS IS OLD HIPI, THE INDIAN CHIEF...

... HIS PEOPLE BELIEVE THAT HE CAN "READ" FACES.

JUST A SUPERSTITION, OF COURSE.

W... WHAT DID HE SAY?

OH... THAT YOU HAVE NO FEAR, THAT YOU ARE NOT STUCK-UP AND THAT YOU KNOW HOW TO LAUGH.

LATER...

HO... OOONK!
HO... OOONK!

WHAT'S OUR MISSIONARY DOING?!!

HONK!

EVERY WEEKDAY, WE BLOW A COWHORN TO CALL THE CHILDREN TO SCHOOL ...

... BUT WE USUALLY HAVE TO GO AND FETCH THEM FROM THEIR CABINS!

SUNDAY MORNING.

HOOONK!

... AND NOW, THE LORD'S PRAYER:

Sunday, A

"OUR FATHER, WHO ART IN HEAVEN..."

THOSE DESKS ARE ALMOST EMPTY ...

THAT'S THE MEN'S SIDE ...

THEY MUST WEAR A CLEAN SHIRT AND TROUSERS TO ATTEND THE SERVICE ...

... BUT MOST ARE TOO POOR TO BUY GOOD CLOTHES.

TIME TO BEGIN WORK...

HELLO...

MAY I...?

THE LARGE CEDAR HOUSE WAS HOME TO SEVERAL FAMILIES. EACH FAMILY HAD ITS OWN FIRE.

EVERYTHING WAS BLACKENED WITH SOOT. SMOKE TEASED MY EYES AND THROAT.

SOME OF THE OLD PEOPLE FEARED THAT I WAS IMPRISONING THEIR SOULS IN MY PAINTINGS ...

THERE WAS THE RAIN, THE SMELL OF ROTTING FISH ON THE SHORE AND THE MOSQUITOES, BUT MY DESIRE TO PAINT WAS STILL STRONG ...

THE CHILDREN BECAME MY DEAREST FRIENDS.

KLEE WYCK!

KLEE WYCK!

KLEE WYCK?

... "KLEE WYCK:" "THE-LAUGHING-ONE," THAT'S WHAT THEY CALLED ME ...

ONE DAY ...

ZZZRR...

HELLO ...!

ZZZ...

I... I WOULD LIKE TO GO TO THE OTHER SIDE OF THE BEACH.

ZZZRR...
ZZRR...
ZZZRR...

THE MAN SMILED AT ME AND SPOKE IN HIS LANGUAGE ... WE COULDN'T UNDERSTAND EACH OTHER.

RRR...
ZZZRR...

NODDING AND LAUGHING TOGETHER, I SAT BESIDE THE OLD MAN SAWING ...

ZZZRR...

... POINTING TO THE SUN AND TO THE SEA, THE EAGLES IN THE AIR AND THE CROWS ON THE BEACH ...

... AS IF TIME DID NOT MATTER ANYMORE.

After learning the rudiments of painting in Victoria, Emily studied art in both San Francisco and London. But living in such a big, bustling city as London was a difficult and painful experience for her. She became ill and had to rest in a hospital for several months. After a few years back in Canada, however, Emily packed up again and, accompanied by her sister Alice, set off for France.

AUTUMN IN FRANCE

PARIS, FRANCE, SEPTEMBER 1910.

NON, NON, NON! MADEMOISELLE...

... I WANT YOU TO EXPRESS THE SHEER BEAUTY OF THE HUMAN BODY.

I CAN'T... ALL THAT NAKED FLESH IS JUST TOO DISGUSTING!

PUSH YOURSELF! SCRAPE AND TRY AGAIN!

BUT... I HAVE AND I HAVE AND I **HAVE**!

THESE FRENCH TEACHERS ARE ALWAYS TELLING ME THE SAME THING ...

WHERE'S THE LITTLE CANADIAN?

SHE LEFT FOR HOME, TEARS STREAMING DOWN HER CHEEKS, MONSIEUR...

TOO BAD ...

YES, TOO BAD INDEED...

... SEE HOW MUCH BETTER HER PICTURE IS NOW.

THAT LADY HAS THE MAKINGS OF A PAINTER, BUT SHE MUST HURT TO PAINT WELL.

MEANWHILE ...

SO MANY STAIRS ...

THERE YOU ARE, MILLIE. HOW WAS YOUR DAY?

SLAM!

Bon-jour Ma-dame, je vou-drais...

... un ki-lo de carot-tes...

ENOUGH!

13

MILLIE!?? HOW **DARE** YOU ...

... I'M YOUR OLDER SISTER AND I THINK I DESERVE A LITTLE MORE RESPECT!

ALICE, I'M THIRTY-EIGHT YEARS OLD! I DON'T NEED ANYBODY TO TELL ME WHAT TO DO!!!

DAYS WENT BY ...

PARIS IS SUCH A BEAUTIFUL CITY ...

WHAT'S WRONG WITH YOU, MILLIE? YOU DON'T EVEN TRY TO LEARN FRENCH.

HOW ABOUT TEA AT THE AMERICAN STUDENT HOSTEL? WE COULD MEET SOME FRIENDS THERE ...

ALL I CARE ABOUT IS ART, ART, **ART!**

THE LOUVRE MUSEUM.

... THE CATALOGUE SAYS THAT IT'S A MASTERPIECE OF CLASSICAL DUTCH PAINTING ...

YOU COULD SAY SOMETHING, MILLIE!

BORING! THAT'S WHAT ALL THIS DUSTY STUFF IS. I WANT TO SEE THE "NEW ART!"

HARRY GIBB, A "MODERN" PAINTER, HAD MOVED FROM ENGLAND TO PARIS SEVERAL YEARS BEFORE.

... I'VE BEEN LOOKING FORWARD TO SEEING YOU AGAIN, MR. GIBB. AND YOUR PAINTINGS, TOO.

... I KNOW TOO WELL WHAT IT MEANS TO BE A FOREIGNER IN PARIS ...

PLEASE... TELL ME ABOUT THIS "NEW ART"...

I'M NOT EXACTLY SURE WHAT "NEW ART" MEANS, BUT ...

... PARIS IS BURSTING WITH TALENTED ARTISTS FROM ALL OVER EUROPE: SPANISH, ITALIANS, GERMANS, RUSSIANS ...

... WHO HAVE DECIDED THAT THEY ARE FINISHED WITH TRADITIONAL ART ...

MILLIE, THESE PICTURES ARE REVOLTING!

SOME FRIENDS OF MINE RUN A GALLERY NOT FAR FROM HERE... WOULD YOU LIKE TO VISIT?

IN THE GALLERY.

THIS IS A MATISSE ... BRAQUE, MODIGLIANI ...

PICASSO... SEE HOW HE'S USING AFRICAN ART FORMS IN HIS WORK.

CÉZANNE, LÉGER, CHAGALL, DUCHAMP...

EMILY, ARE YOU ALL RIGHT?

SORRY, I... I'M FEELING DIZZY ...

AMERICAN STUDENT HOSTEL INFIRMARY, PARIS, DECEMBER 1910.

A VISITOR FOR YOU, MISS.

MILLIE ...

... HOW'S YOUR HEADACHE?

ALICE ... I'M SO WEAK ...

YOU NEED TO REST. YOU DROVE YOURSELF TOO HARD.

I DON'T WANT TO STAY HERE ... TAKE ME BACK HOME ... PLEASE!

DOCTOR ...

THERE'S SOMETHING ABOUT BIG CITIES THAT YOUR SISTER CAN'T STAND. IT'S JUST LIKE PUTTING A PINE TREE IN A POT ...

JANUARY.

I THINK YOU WERE RIGHT, ALICE ...

... MY PAINTING IS NOT GOING ANYWHERE ...

... I FEEL AS THOUGH I'VE GONE STALE.

16

Even though she felt that her creative well springs had run dry, two of Emily's paintings were accepted by Paris's renowned Salon d'Automne. Following her illness in Paris, Emily moved to the French countryside where she regained her strength and energy before returning home. Back in Canada she opened a studio where she gave art classes to children and embarked on her sketching expeditions once more. But her new work was too bold for many people and, unable to make a living from her art, she gradually gave up painting.

SILHOUETTE

VICTORIA, BRITISH COLUMBIA, SEPTEMBER 1927.

GOOD MORNING.

... 'MORNING.

POOR WOMAN.

WHAT A PECULIAR NEIGHBOR WE HAVE ...

LOOK HERE, MY BABIES, WHAT MOTHER HAS BROUGHT YOU FROM THE BUTCHER SHOP!

RRRING! RRRING!

WHO'S THAT?

MISS CARR, THIS IS ERIC BROWN, DIRECTOR OF THE NATIONAL GALLERY ...

... I'M HERE TO PREPARE AN EXHIBITION ON WEST COAST ART. I HAVE A BIT OF TIME LEFT AND I'D LIKE TO SEE YOUR PICTURES OF INDIAN TOTEM POLES ...

WELL... I NEVER HEARD ABOUT THAT GALLERY, SIR... ALL THOSE OLD PAINTINGS ARE STORED AWAY, AND I DOUBT ...

... YES, I'LL BE HERE ALL DAY.

18

ALL THIS DUST ...

KNOCK KNOCK!

I'M COMING!

HERE ARE THE PAINTINGS.

PLEASE FORGIVE THE MESS, FEW PEOPLE VISIT ME THESE DAYS.

I DON'T REALLY PAINT ANYMORE... I RAISE SHEEP DOGS AND SELL RUGS AND CLAY POTS TO THE TOURISTS...

MISS CARR ...

... THIS IS SOME OF THE MOST ASTONISHING WORK I HAVE SEEN IN YEARS.

LATER THAT AFTERNOON...

I'LL HAVE THOSE FIFTY PAINTINGS SHIPPED TO OTTAWA EARLY NEXT MONTH...

... AND, OF COURSE, I WANT YOU TO COME FOR THE SHOW. WE'LL SEND YOU A TICKET FOR THE TRAIN.

FIFTY OF MY PICTURES! ME GO EAST! WHO DID YOU SAY YOU WERE?

OPENING RECEPTION OF THE "EXHIBITION OF CANADIAN WEST COAST ART", NATIONAL GALLERY, OTTAWA, DECEMBER 1927.

WHO CAN PAINT WITH SUCH A FURY? EVEN OUR WORK LOOKS TAME IN COMPARISON!

THIS, MY DEAR LISMER, IS A DISCOVERY I'M VERY PROUD OF...

OH, THERE SHE IS... EMILY!

DON'T BE IMPRESSED BY THESE WELL-DRESSED GENTLEMEN. THEY ARE SIMPLY TALENTED ARTISTS, LIKE YOU!

... YOU'VE MET ARTHUR LISMER AND A.Y. JACKSON OF THE GROUP OF SEVEN. AND THIS IS EDWIN HOLGATE...

IMPRESSIVE WORK, MISS CARR.

COME TO OUR STUDIOS IN TORONTO BEFORE YOU RETURN HOME!

20

TUXEDO HOTEL, TORONTO, DECEMBER 1927.

... IF ONLY I'D HEARD OF THEM EARLIER ...

... TOMORROW, I WILL SEE LAWREN HARRIS AGAIN, ANOTHER MEMBER OF THE GROUP ...

THE NEXT DAY ...

"STUDIO BUILDING" ON SEVERN STREET.

KNOCK KNOCK!

MISS CARR... PLEASE COME IN!

IT'S WONDERFUL TO SEE YOU AGAIN.

MY STUDIO...

I AM TRYING TO REVEAL THE SPIRITUAL TRUTH ...

... CONCEALED INSIDE A TREE, A ROCK, A MOUNTAIN.

THERE IS A UNIVERSAL SENSE OF ORDER, UNITY AND PROPORTION ...

... IN EVERYTHING AROUND US.

ART AND RELIGION ARE ONE.

MISS ...

I AM SORRY ... YOU MUST BE TIRED OF ALL THIS TALK.

HOW CAN I THANK YOU? I HAVE LEARNED MORE THIS AFTERNOON ...

... THAN IN MY ENTIRE LIFE! I MUST START PAINTING AGAIN ...

Emily's meeting with the artists who formed the Group of Seven – and in particular with Lawren Harris, with whom she corresponded for many years – was a tremendous revelation to her. In her mid-fifties she now no longer felt alone in her artistic and spiritual quest and, despite failing health, she embarked on a period of extraordinary creativity.

BELOVED OF THE SKY

VICTORIA, BRITISH COLUMBIA, JULY 1933.

COME ON, WOO ... LET'S GO CHECK THE MAIL.

A LETTER FROM LAWREN...

" ... YOUR LAST PAINTINGS ARE A VERY GREAT ADVANCE ON YOUR PREVIOUS WORK. IT IS AS IF YOUR IDEAS, VISIONS, FEELINGS, WERE COMING TO PRECISE EXPRESSION ... "

" ... KEEP ON... DO WHAT YOU FEEL LIKE DOING MOST... GET THE ESSENCE FROM NATURE HERSELF, GIVE IT NEW FORM AND INTENSITY ... "

DEAR, DEAR LAWREN... WHAT A GREAT FRIEND.

GOOD MORNING, MILLIE ...

ALICE! HOW ABOUT A CUP OF TEA?

OH... HAVE YOU SEEN MY "ELEPHANT?"

A... AN **ELEPHANT!** BUT... DON'T YOU ALREADY HAVE ENOUGH PETS ?!!

ALICE! "ELEPHANT" IS THE NAME I'VE GIVEN TO THIS OLD TRAILER ...

I BOUGHT IT WITH MONEY FROM MY PAINTINGS ...

... I'VE ALWAYS DREAMED OF LIVING LIKE A GYPSY!

MILLIE, IS THERE A DAY WHEN YOU'LL SIMPLY LIVE LIKE ... AN ADULT?

AN ADULT ...? SPARE ME, GOD!

LATER...

... THINK ABOUT THE LIVES OF OUR OLDER SISTERS ...

... THEY OBEYED OUR PARENTS, THEY OBEYED THEIR TEACHERS, THEY NEVER BROKE A RULE ... AND NOW THEY ARE DEAD.

... AS A WOMAN, AND AS AN ARTIST, I HAVE HAD TO FACE MANY OBSTACLES ...

... BUT AT LEAST I AM FREE.

SOMETIMES, I WONDER ... IF YOU WERE NOT RIGHT AFTER ALL, MILLIE.

WHO KNOWS, ALICE ... WHO KNOWS?

25

TWO OR THREE TIMES A YEAR, THE "ELEPHANT" WAS HAULED TO A NEW LOCATION WHERE EMILY COULD PAINT AND ENJOY THE WILDERNESS.

... HERE I WAS, FAR FROM THE CIVILIZED WORLD, ALL MY TROUBLES LEFT AT HOME, SURROUNDED ONLY BY MY BELOVED ANIMALS AND THE SOOTHING, ETERNAL BEAUTY OF MOTHER NATURE.

I BATHED IN A NEARBY BROOK AND ATE LITTLE, OFTEN FASTING FOR DAYS ON ORANGE JUICE AND VERY LIGHT FOOD ...

... IT WAS AS IF A NEW, UNKNOWN ENERGY HAD STARTED FLOWING THROUGH MY VEINS.

DAY AFTER DAY, I CARRIED MY DRAWING BOARD AND BRUSHES INTO THE WOODS AND SAT AMONG THE HUGE CEDARS, STARING AND PAINTING ...

THE EVENINGS WERE DEVOTED TO WRITING. THE ONLY SOUND WAS THE GENTLE SWAYING OF THE TREES BEYOND THE WINDOW.

I THOUGHT THAT FINALLY I HAD FOUND HAPPINESS ...

... UNTIL A TERRIBLE THING HAPPENED.

WOO!

... YOU CAN'T LEAVE ME LIKE THIS!

ALL EVENING, I HUNG OVER MY MONKEY AS SHE LAY ACROSS A HOT WATER BOTTLE ON MY LAP ...

... I WASHED INSIDE HER THROAT AS FAR AS I COULD REACH WITH GASOLINE RAGS.

... HOW DID YOU KNOW THAT GREEN IS THE DEADLIEST COLOR?

LATER THAT NIGHT, I HAD A STRANGE DREAM ...

... I WAS STANDING BESIDE A HILL, AN ORDINARY HILL COVERED WITH TREES ...

... AND THEN THE HILLSIDE BEGAN TO MOVE, TO BREATHE LIKE A PERSON, HEAVY WITH SAP, BURNING GREEN IN EVERY LEAF ...

THE NEXT MORNING, THE LIGHT WAS SO PURE THAT I DECIDED TO GO OUT AND PAINT.

WANDERING THROUGH THE TANGLES OF DENSE, LUSH UNDERGROWTH, IT WAS AS IF MY DREAM AND REALITY HAD BECOME ONE ...

... I FELT THE NEARNESS OF GOD, THE INVISIBLE SPIRIT INHABITING THE LEAVES OF THE TREES, THE ROCKS UNDER MY FEET, THE CLOUDS IN THE SKY ...

... EVERY PLANE, EVERY SCRAP OF THE UNIVERSE SEEMED TO ADVANCE AND RECEDE, TO MOVE, SWIRL AND DANCE IN A CONTINUOUS CELEBRATION OF JOY ...

... THE FULL,
PURE JOY OF LIFE.

THAT EVENING ...

WOO?

THERE YOU ARE AGAIN... ALIVE!